TREE HOUSE TOWN

TREE HOUSE TOWN

MISKA MILES

Illustrated by
EMILY McCULLY

An Atlantic Monthly Press Book
BOSTON   Little, Brown and Company   TORONTO

FIRST EDITION

T 10/74

Library of Congress Cataloging in Publication Data

Miles, Miska.
  Tree house town.
  "An Atlantic Monthly Press book."
  I. McCully, Emily Arnold, illus. II. Title.
PZ7.M5944Tr   [E]   74-3358
ISBN 0-316-56971-2

ATLANTIC-LITTLE, BROWN BOOKS
ARE PUBLISHED BY
LITTLE, BROWN AND COMPANY
IN ASSOCIATION WITH
THE ATLANTIC MONTHLY PRESS

*Published simultaneously in Canada
by Little, Brown & Company (Canada) Limited*

PRINTED IN THE UNITED STATES OF AMERICA

For
Deanna Lyn Canales

Mouse lived in a tiny cave under the root of a big oak tree that grew on Green Hill.

When it was day, he curled up in his cave and went to sleep. At night he came creeping out and ate good weed seeds, and wild berries when he could find them.

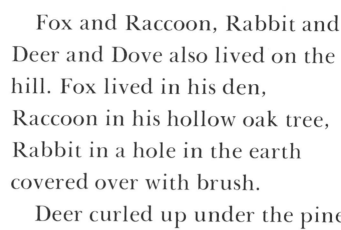

Fox and Raccoon, Rabbit and
Deer and Dove also lived on the
hill. Fox lived in his den,
Raccoon in his hollow oak tree,
Rabbit in a hole in the earth
covered over with brush.

Deer curled up under the pine
branches. Dove perched
wherever he liked, whenever he
liked.

Two girls came up Green Hill, carrying lunch sacks.

"This is a great place for a tree house," Josie said.

"Where?" said Ella.

"Right in that tree," said Josie. "We'll build one."

"Let's eat first," said Ella. "Then we can go home and get some wood and a hammer."

"And a saw and some nails," said Josie.

"And some cookies," said Ella.

They went home and came back, again and again, for rope and boards and boxes and cookies.

And as they worked, the forest was filled with the sounds of their building.

Bang — bang — bang —
Crack — crack —
Thump —

Mouse huddled in his cave —
afraid.

When it was night and
everything was quiet, Mouse
came out. He ran here and there,
here and there, under the tree
house.

Fox came to sniff at the
footprints under the tree house.
He barked and trotted away over
the hill.

Mouse held a bit of cracker in
his front paws.

Now, on the hill were left only
Raccoon and Rabbit, Deer and
Dove. And Mouse —

The next day, Josie said to Ella, "Let's show our house to the rest of the kids."

Carlos and Rosita came to look at it.

"We'll build one, too," Rosita said. "We'll build it here."

Raccoon huddled in his own
oak tree, and shivered with the
sound of hammer against nail.
And soon there was another
tree house, made of old shutters
and screens.

Raccoon came down from his oak tree. He didn't stop at all. Away he walked to the other side of the hill.

Now, on the hill were left only Rabbit and Deer, Dove and Mouse.

Up the hill came Susie and Elizabeth Ann with their big, old dog.

They started building a house using leftover pieces from the first houses and an old chalkboard.

"Ouch," said Susie. "I stepped in a hole."

"Maybe a rabbit hole," said Elizabeth Ann.

The dog ran everywhere and barked.

He found Rabbit's den and sniffed at it. Then he pushed his way through the brush and into the pines. Deer leaped out and dashed away.

When the moon was high, Rabbit slowly poked his head out of his den. He crept outside, and quickly hopped away to the forest on the other side of the hill.

Mouse came from his den and darted under the tree houses, zigzagging here and there.

Now on the hill were only Dove and Mouse.

Angela and Tom and their small brother, Jackson, came to the hill.

Jackson carried their cat.

When he set the cat down on the ground, it scurried up into the treetop.

Angela and Tom and Jackson looked at the tree houses.

"Beautiful," said Angela.

"We'll build one," Tom said.

Dove flew out of the treetop,
and away over the hill.

Now on Green Hill, there was
only Mouse.

Other boys and girls came and they worked, building and eating and building. And the forest was filled with their noise.

Bang — bang —

Crack — crack — crack —

And soon a town was there on the hill.

On the other side of the hill
live Fox and Raccoon, Rabbit,
Deer and Dove.

Fox has a new den. Raccoon
found a hollow tree. Rabbit has a
hole in the ground, Deer is safe
in a pine grove, and Dove
perches here and there.

nostril *nose* *tongue* *teeth*

tasting

touching

seeing

smelling

hearing

cheek

chin

5

BABY'S
Things

bootees

blanket

pins

high chair

rattle

potty

cotton balls

soft toy

monitors

BIB

oatmeal

milk

cheese

meat

rice

pasta

honey

salad

17

PARTY
Food

muffin

fried chicken

potato chips

fruit tart

pretzels

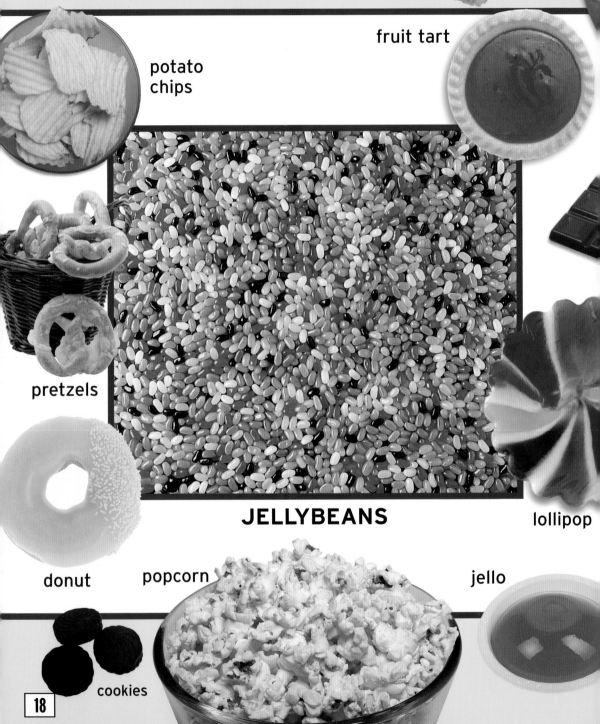

JELLYBEANS

lollipop

donut

popcorn

jello

cookies

18

marshmallows

candy
cane

nuts

cake

chocolate

soda

pizza

hamburger

fries

19

Fruit

raspberry

cherries

kiwi fruit

tomato

avocado

ORANGES

grapefruit

pear

banana

olives

20 apricot

mangoes

mandarin
orange

dates

strawberry

pineapple

apple

lemon

watermelon

grapes

peaches

21

Vegetables

asparagus

onion

cabbages

leeks

carrots

SWEET CORN

cauliflower

radish

spinach

mushrooms

rhubarb

broccoli

zucchini

parsnip

beet

lettuce

green onions

turnip

potatoes

eggplant

peas

23

Plants

acorns

fern

grass

holly

ivy

blossom

cactus

LEAVES

seedling

pine cone

moss

trunk

bark

bottlebrush

wattle

gum flowers

palm tree

oak leaves

weeping willow

maple

flytrap

potted plants

25

Flowers

pansy

violet

bouquet

daisy

chrysanthemum

orchid

bluebell

SUNFLOWER

tulip

cornflower

knotweed

gardenia

26

zinnia

carnation

hibiscus

iris

marigold

rose

lily

freesia

gerbera

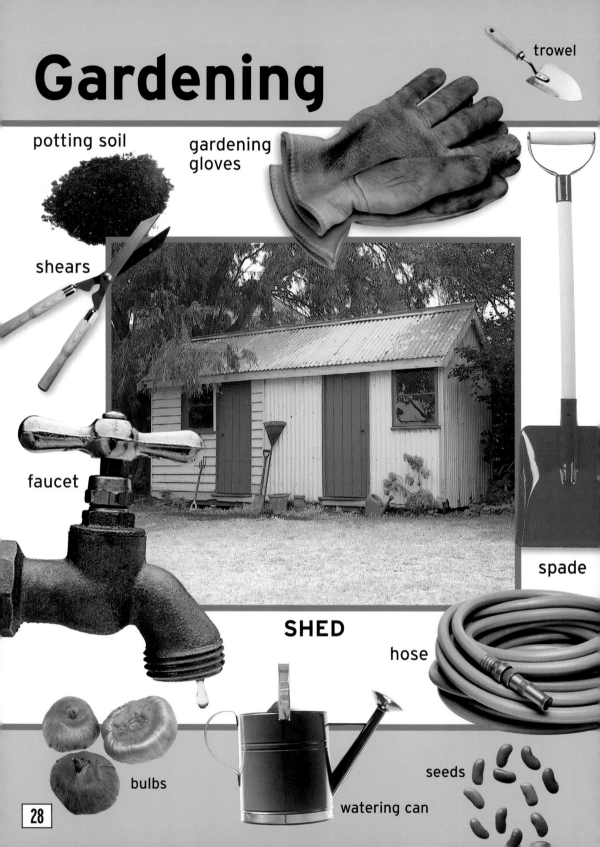

Gardening

trowel

potting soil

gardening gloves

shears

faucet

spade

SHED

hose

bulbs

seeds

watering can

compost bin

flowerpots

clippers

gardening hat

wheelbarrow

lawnmower

rake

shovel

weeds

rock

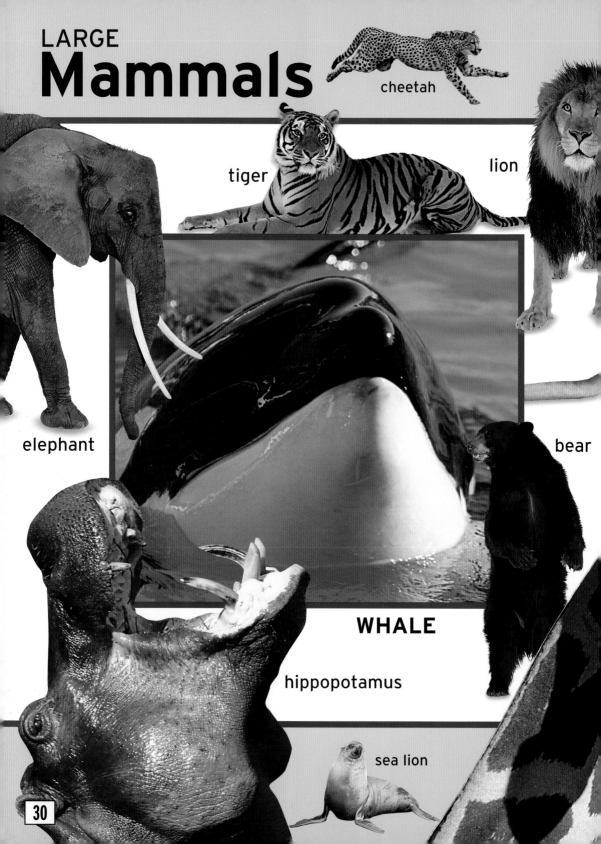

LARGE Mammals

cheetah

tiger

lion

elephant

bear

WHALE

hippopotamus

sea lion

rhinoceros

polar bear

deer

monkey

dolphins

kangaroo

camel

leopard

giraffe

chimpanzee

puma

gorilla

moose

SMALL
Mammals

hedgehog

rat

squirrel

otter

raccoon

meerkats

BADGER

koala

opossum

fox

echidna

skunk

wombat

chipmunk

hare

possum

wolverine

bat

beaver

Tasmanian devil

armadillo

33

Birds

emu

pigeon

owl

kingfisher

puffin

parrot

ALBATROSS

eagle

macaw

pelican

ostrich

falcon

hawk

lovebird

flamingo

crane

peacock

toucan

swans

vulture

woodpecker

REPTILES AND
Amphibians

bullfrog

alligator

skink

iguana

gecko

KOMODO DRAGON

cobra

terrapin

tortoise

toad

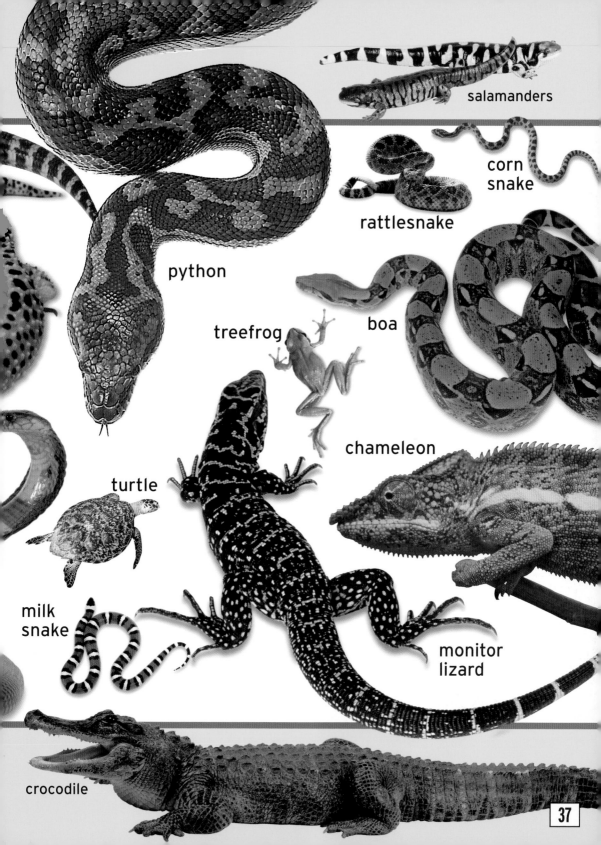

salamanders

corn
snake

rattlesnake

python

treefrog

boa

chameleon

turtle

milk
snake

monitor
lizard

crocodile

37

WATER
Animals

puffer
fish

lobster

herrings

tuna

oysters

shrimp

angelfish

stingray

JELLYFISH

seadragon

coral

shark

damsel fish

cod

sardines

salmon

sea horse

starfish

catfish

crab

eel

pike

39

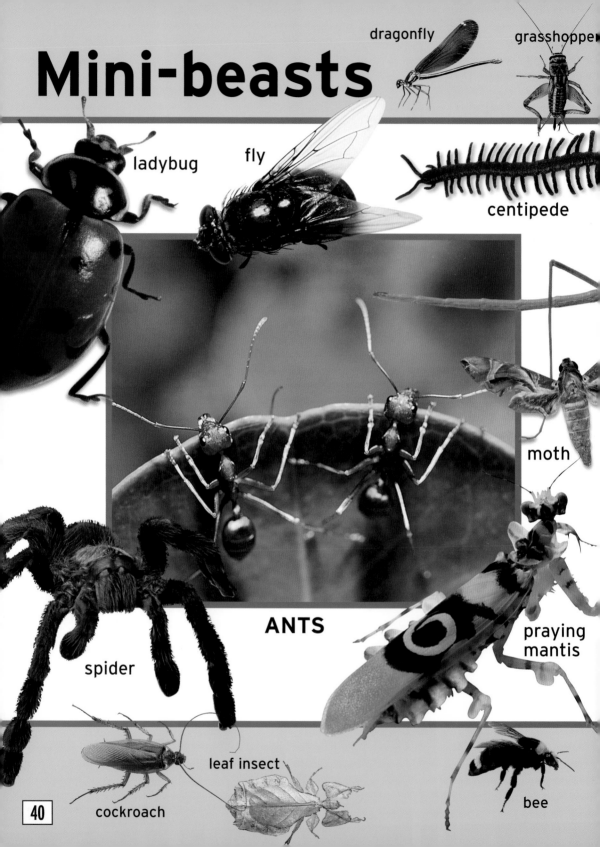

Mini-beasts

dragonfly

grasshopper

ladybug

fly

centipede

moth

ANTS

spider

praying mantis

leaf insect

cockroach

bee

40

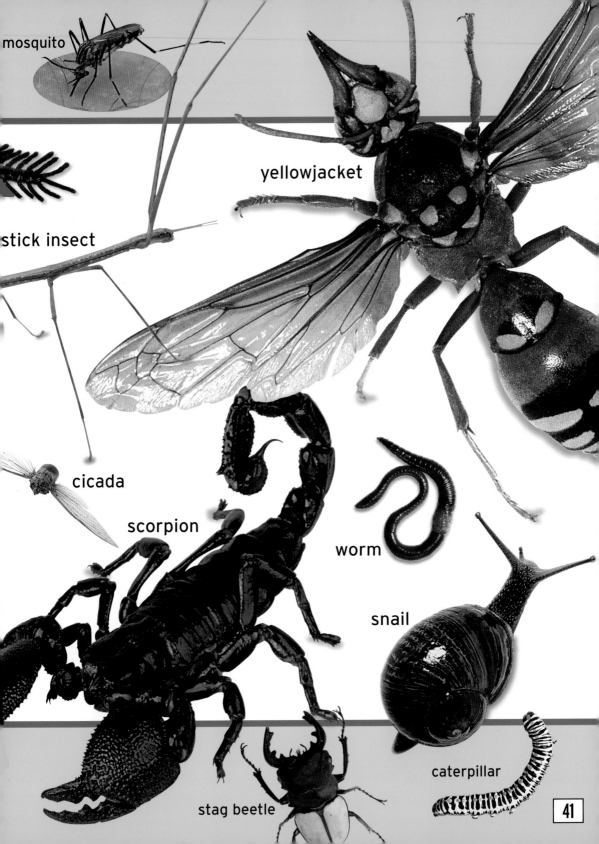

mosquito

yellowjacket

stick insect

cicada

scorpion

worm

snail

stag beetle

caterpillar

41

ANIMAL
Bodies

hoof

feathers

horn

wings

FANGS

fur

tail

spines

talons

whiskers

scales

paw

claws

gill

mane

snout

antlers

pouch

tusks

fin

beak

43

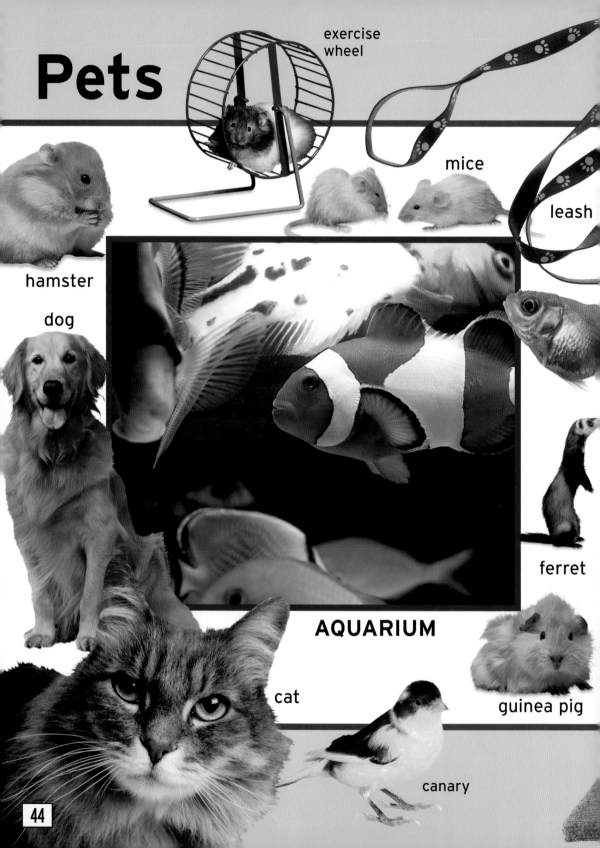

Pets

exercise wheel

mice

leash

hamster

dog

AQUARIUM

ferret

guinea pig

cat

canary

44

pony

doghouse

collar

pet toy

rabbit

goldfish

cage

stable

saddle

scratching post

pet bed

45

A House

door knocker

mailbox

balcony

window

curtain

lawn

doormat

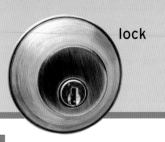
lock

wall
blind

door

porch

gutter

bricks

fence

garage
drive

roof

trash
can

doorknob

IN THE
Bedroom

dresser

night-light

photo frame

alarm clock

toy box

quilt

pillow

BED

trophy

books

The Folk of the Faraway Tree

bathrobe

wardrobe

48

slippers

rocking horse

mattress

pajamas

hat rack

teddy bear

rug

poster

49

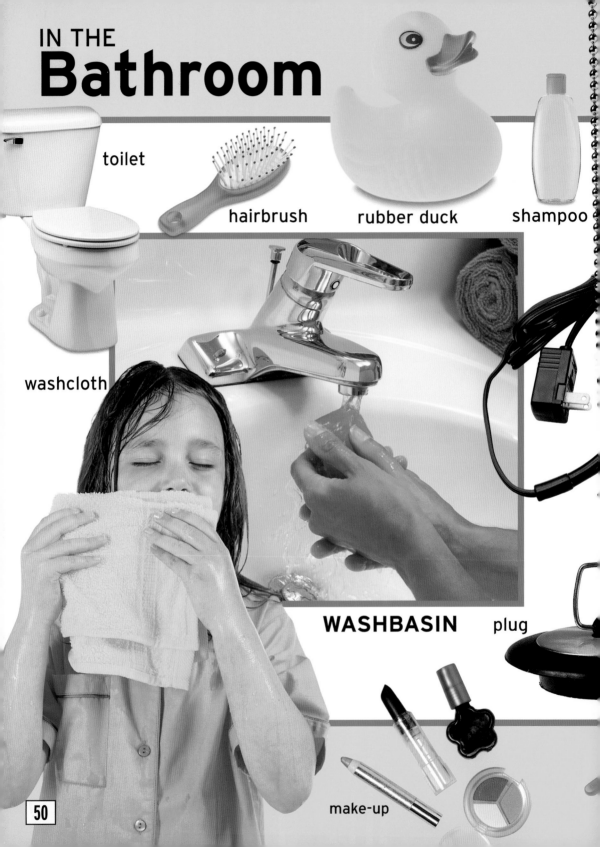

IN THE
Bathroom

toilet

hairbrush

rubber duck

shampoo

washcloth

WASHBASIN

plug

make-up

medicine

tissues

comb

toothpaste

toilet paper

shower

hairdryer

mirror

towel

bathtub

toothbrush

soap

bubble bath

51

IN THE
Family Room

video recorder

coffee table

lamp

remote
control

rocking
chair

cushion

BOOKSHELF

vase

television

52

compact disc

video cassettes

picture

carpet

beanbag

games table

coasters

headphones

couch

newspaper

stereo

magazines

53

IN THE
Kitchen

juicer

kitchen
scales

range

electric
mixer

cooktop

apron

toaster

stool

BENCHTOP

refrigerator

food
processor

54

table

cutting board

chair

breadmaker

kettle

jar

sink

cookbook

dishwasher

microwave oven

55

IN THE
Cabinet

bowl

saucepan

cake pan

dishwashing
liquid

plate

PLATTER

sponge

teapot

cup

dishtowel

rubber gloves

rolling pin

wooden spoon

glass

knife

fork

spoon

tray

egg beater

fry pan

jug

57

IN THE
Study

envelope

desk

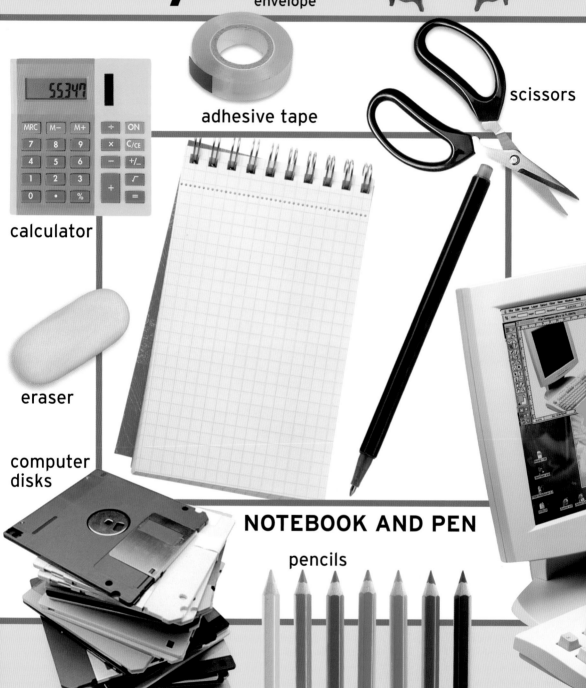

adhesive tape

scissors

calculator

eraser

computer
disks

NOTEBOOK AND PEN

pencils

58

dictionary

stapler

diary

telephone

office chair

paper clip

sharpener

paper

computer

ruler

glue

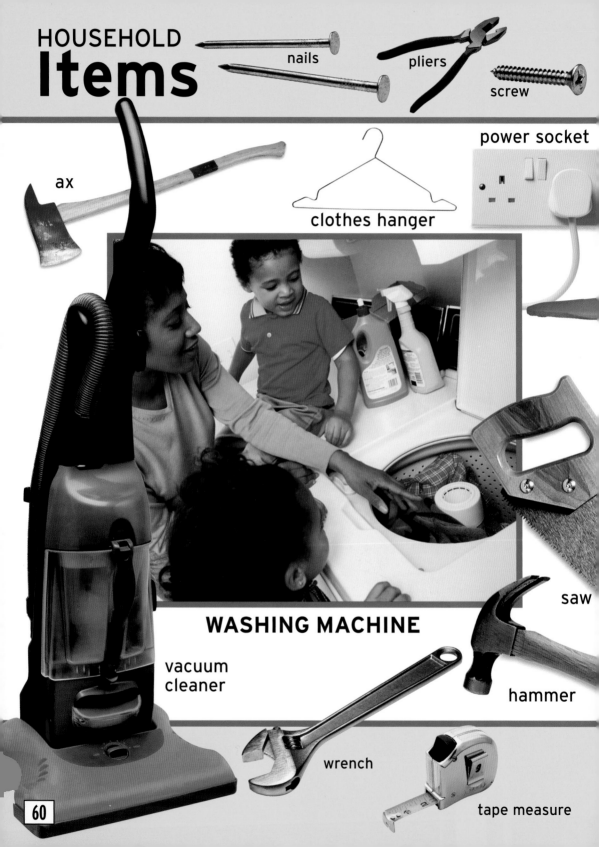

HOUSEHOLD
Items

nails

pliers

screw

ax

clothes hanger

power socket

saw

WASHING MACHINE

vacuum cleaner

hammer

wrench

tape measure

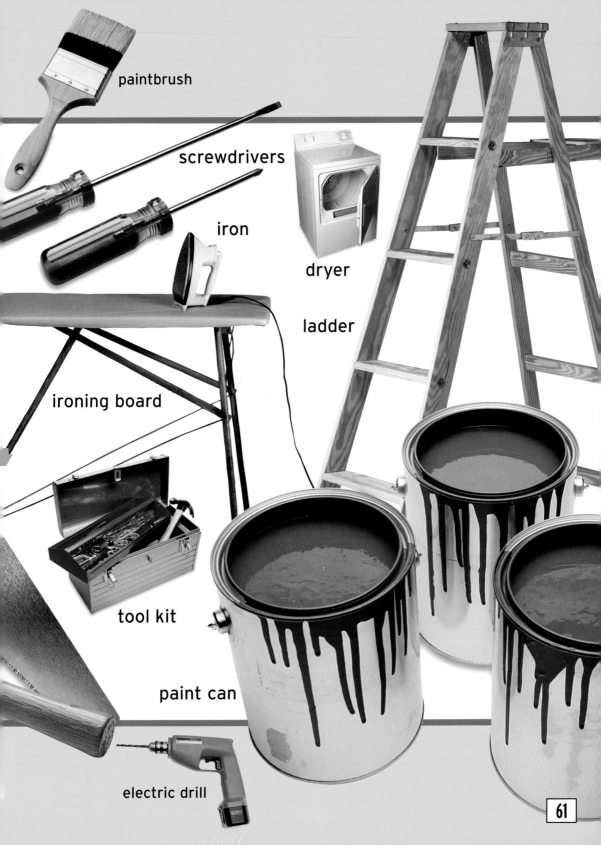

paintbrush

screwdrivers

iron

dryer

ladder

ironing board

tool kit

paint can

electric drill

Birthday Party

candy

banne

greeting card

plastic cup

BIRTHDAY CAKE

wrapping paper

gifts

candles

gift bag

62

streamers

fruit drink

bow

party whistles

invitation

straws

badge

party hat

birthday girl

mask

friends

party game

63

Fancy Dress

wand

bumblebee

glitter

Little
Bo Peep

king

butterfly

mouse

octopus

flower

kitty

tiara

fairy wings

sea lion

costume

bunny

starfish

puppy

calf

pirate

wig

clown

Toys

dice

dollhouse

dinosaur

wagon

soldier

dragon

PUZZLE

blackboard

cowboy

checkerboard

cube

skipping rope

doll

cards

spaceship

robot

tricycle

blocks

slinky

dominoes

marbles

67

FAVORITE
Things

jewelry

kite

boomerang

money

crayons

piggy
bank

penguin

SEE-SAW

telescope

ukulele

stickers

scarf

68

magnet

quilt

fishing rod

chess set

coconut

Frisbee

tutu

radio

yo-yo

69

SPORTS
Equipment

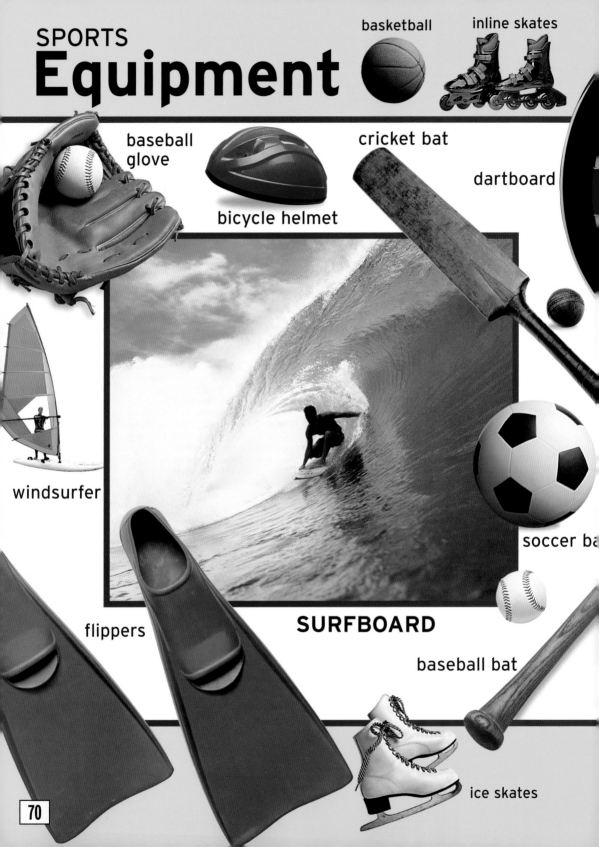

basketball

inline skates

baseball glove

bicycle helmet

cricket bat

dartboard

windsurfer

flippers

SURFBOARD

soccer ba

baseball bat

ice skates

whistle

skis

stopwatch

darts

bicycle

30
28
26
24
22
20
18
16
58
56
54
52
50
48
46
4
15
12
9
6
1/10

goggles

wetsuit

tennis racket

football

field hockey
stick

71

MUSICAL
Instruments

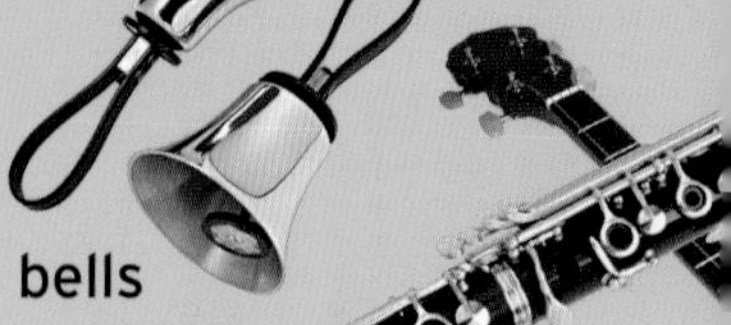

bells

flute

clarinet

triang

harp

ACOUSTIC GUITAR

cello

maracas

xylophone

piano

recorder

accordion

banjo

tambourine

trumpet

cymbals

saxophone

bagpipes

drums

electric guitar

violin

73

ON THE
Farm

scarecrow

horse

foal

hen

chick

pig

donkey

duck

SHEEPDOG

lamb

rooster

74

tractor

cow

farmer

farmhouse

goats

sheep

field

goose

hay bale

gate

75

AT THE
Beach

ice cream

beach ball

deckchair

seaweed

sunscreen

ROCK POOL

swim ring

shells

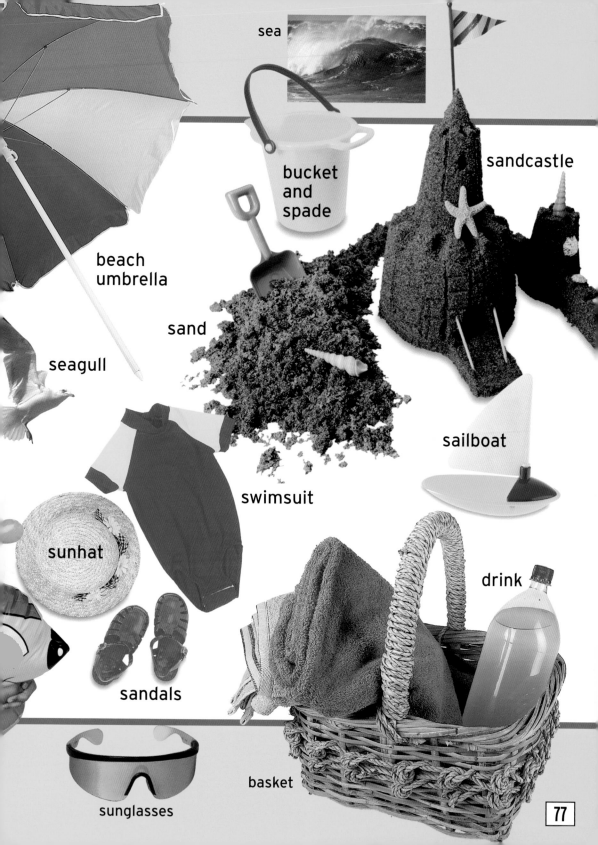

sea

bucket
and
spade

sandcastle

beach
umbrella

sand

seagull

sailboat

swimsuit

sunhat

drink

sandals

basket

sunglasses

Camping

hiking boot

sleeping mat

trail mix

Swiss army knife

binoculars

thermos

gas lamp

camping stove

MAP

compass

matches

rope

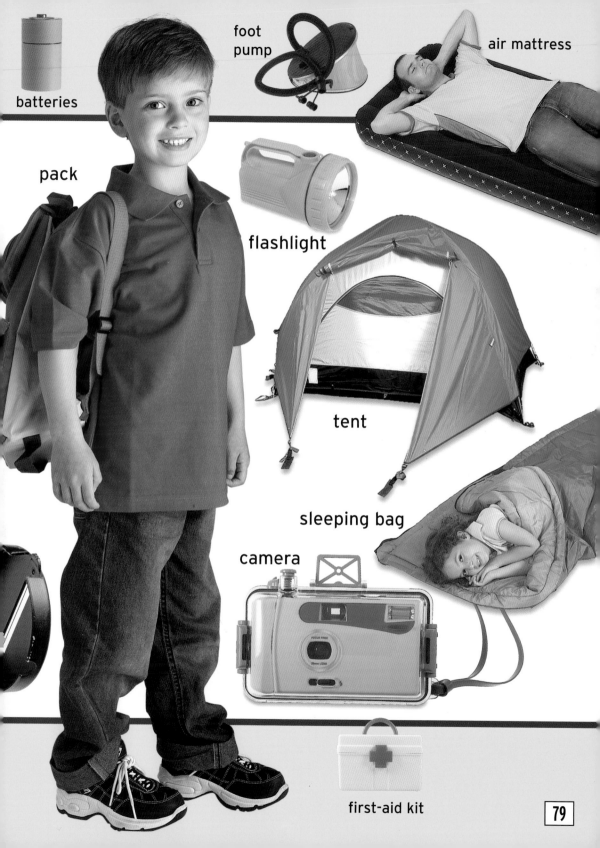

batteries

foot
pump

air mattress

pack

flashlight

tent

sleeping bag

camera

first-aid kit

79

Transport

helicopter

bus

ambulance

cab

wheelchair

BOAT

motorcycle

fire engine

scooter

jet ski

car

ship

airplane

skateboard

truck

yacht

hot-air balloon

racing car

submarine

train

PEOPLE
at Work

electrician

chef

sailor

ballerina

doctor

scientist

artist

decorator

FIREFIGHTERS

detective

82

judge

soccer player

plumber

police officer

boxer

waiter

astronaut

builder

nurse

office worker

teacher

83

Actions

walking

talking

climbing

drawing

hugging

sitting

HIDING

crying

reading

drinking

running

sleeping

playing

cutting

eating

kicking

jumping

reaching

frowning

writing

laughing

85

Opposites

open closed

fat

dry

thin

wet

under

over

push

pull

down

up

young

old

short

long

empty

full

big

clean

small

dirty

87

Numbers

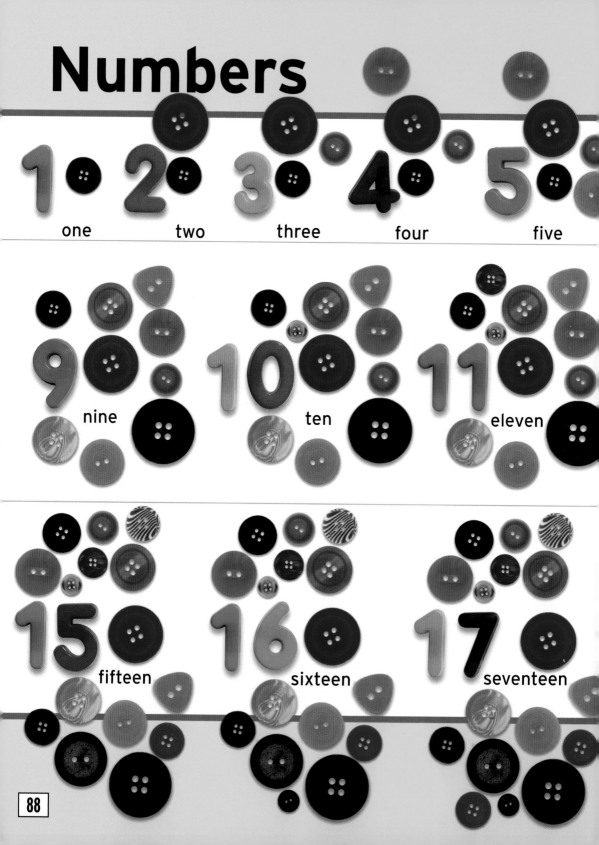

1 one

2 two

3 three

4 four

5 five

9 nine

10 ten

11 eleven

15 fifteen

16 sixteen

17 seventeen

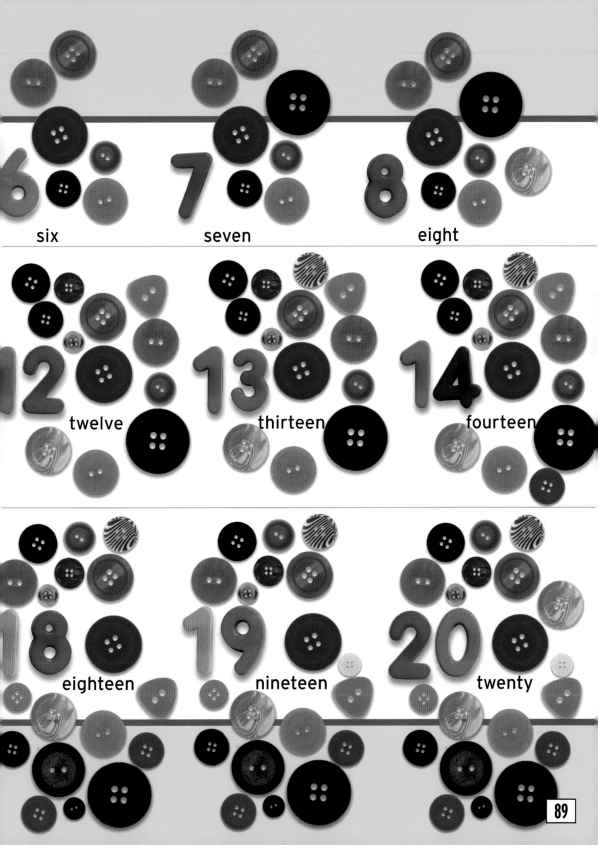

six

seven

eight

twelve

thirteen

fourteen

eighteen

nineteen

twenty

COLORS
and Shapes

yellow

blue

green

gray

orange

purple

white

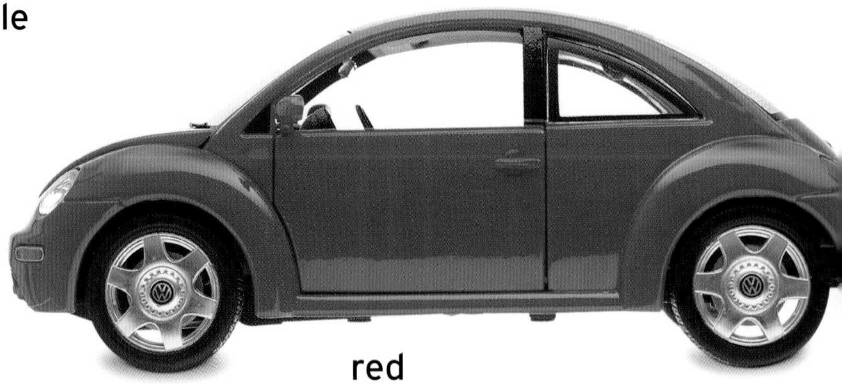

red

brown

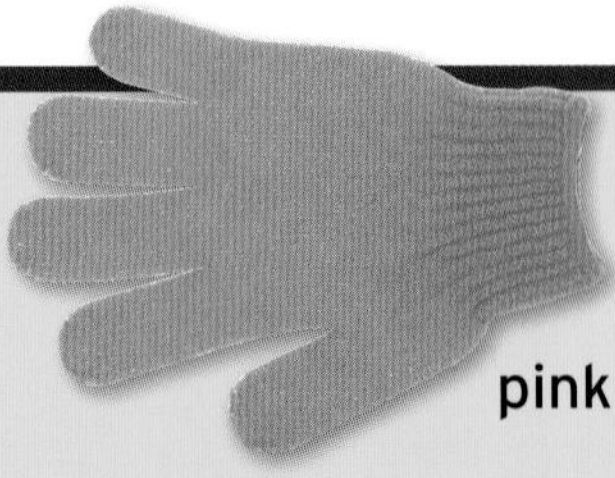

pink

black

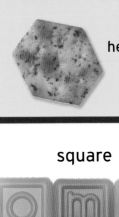
hexagon

crescent

triangle

square

circle

rectangle

heart

diamond

STOP
octagon

star

oval

91

Flags

The Netherlands

Canada

Belgium

Mexico

Philippines

Australia

Singapore

Hungary

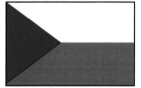
The Czech Republic

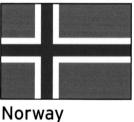
Norway

Poland

South Korea

Finland

United Kingdom

Egypt

Brazil

South Africa

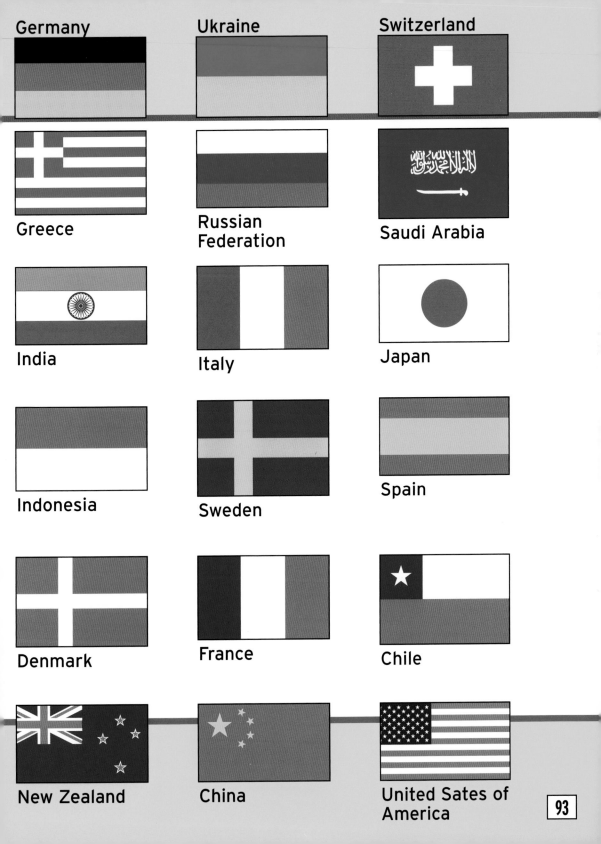

Germany

Ukraine

Switzerland

Greece

Russian Federation

Saudi Arabia

India

Italy

Japan

Indonesia

Sweden

Spain

Denmark

France

Chile

New Zealand

China

United Sates of America

93

THE
Earth and Sky

clouds

Earth

forest

MOUNTAIN

wind

lightning

desert

eclipse

rain

iceberg

river

moon

pond

rainbow

stars

storm

sun

volcano

cave

waterfall

pasture

95